SECOND CHANCES IN SHIMLA

ATUL MOHITE

Contents

CHAPTER ONE

The Return

Meera stepped off the bus, pulling her scarf tighter around her neck as the cold, crisp air of Shimla greeted her. It had been years since she last stood on these familiar streets, yet nothing about the town had changed. The colonial-style buildings, the old church at the top of the hill, and the winding roads still had the same charm that she remembered from her childhood. But this time, it was different. This time, she wasn't here for a holiday. She was back for good.

She glanced around, trying to take it all in. It was a chilly December morning, and the town was slowly waking up, with shopkeepers opening their stores and locals gathering around tea stalls for their first cup of chai. Meera felt a pang of nostalgia as she passed the familiar bookstore her father had owned. It had been the heart of her childhood—an escape, a sanctuary, and a place where she had dreamed of endless possibilities. But now, the shutters were down, and a thin layer of dust had settled over the glass windows.

"Welcome home, Meera," she whispered to herself, trying to muster a smile. It was strange how life had brought her back here after all these years. She had spent a decade in Delhi, building her career in marketing, climbing the corporate ladder, and convincing herself she had outgrown this small hill town. Yet, here she was, with a suitcase in hand and a sense of uncertainty she hadn't felt in a long time.

The decision to return wasn't easy. After her father's passing, there was no one left to look after the bookstore, and she knew it was up to her to keep his legacy alive. It was something she owed him—and perhaps, something she owed herself.

As she made her way to her family home, she couldn't help but feel a mix of anxiety and anticipation. She had been avoiding this place for so long, running away from the memories she had left behind. Memories of a simpler time, of late-night walks under a starry sky, of laughter that echoed through the hills, and of a love that had once meant everything to her.

"Stop it, Meera," she muttered under her breath, shaking off the thought. She was here to focus on the bookstore, not to dwell on the past.

But fate had other plans. Just as she reached the corner of Mall Road, she saw a familiar figure standing outside a small café. He was leaning against the railing, a steaming cup of coffee in his hand, gazing out at the valley below. For a moment, she thought she was imagining it. She hadn't seen him in so long, but there was no mistaking the way he stood, the way his hair fell slightly over his forehead. It was Raj.

Meera froze, her heart skipping a beat. She had known she might run into him someday—Shimla was a small town, after all—but she hadn't expected it to happen so soon. She thought about turning around, walking the other way before he could notice her, but it was too late. Raj looked up, and their eyes met.

For a moment, neither of them moved. It was as if time had stopped, and all the years that had passed melted away. Meera felt a surge of emotions she hadn't allowed herself to feel in years—nostalgia, sadness, and something she couldn't quite place. She took a deep breath and forced herself to smile, even though she wasn't sure if she was ready for this conversation.

"Meera?" Raj's voice was soft, almost hesitant, as if he was afraid she might disappear if he spoke too loudly. He took a step forward, a look of surprise and confusion on his face. "I... I didn't know you were back."

"Just got in," she replied, trying to keep her tone casual, even though her heart was racing. "I'm here to take care of the bookstore."

He nodded, and there was a moment of awkward silence between them. It was strange, standing here, talking to someone who had once been her everything, yet now felt like a stranger. She couldn't help but notice how much he had changed. There were faint lines around his eyes, and his hair was slightly grayer than she remembered. But there was still that same warmth in his gaze, the same kindness that had drawn her to him all those years ago.

"I'm sorry about your dad," Raj said finally, his voice gentle. "He was a good man."

"Thank you," Meera replied, her throat tightening. She had heard those words so many times over the past few months, but hearing them from Raj felt different, more real. "It's been... tough."

"I can imagine," he said softly. "If you need anything, you know where to find me."

She nodded, not trusting herself to speak. There were so many things she wanted to say, so many questions she had, but now wasn't the time. She wasn't ready to reopen old wounds, not yet. Instead, she forced a smile and said, "It's good to see you, Raj."

"You too, Meera," he said, returning her smile, though there was a hint of sadness in his eyes. "Welcome back."

With that, she turned and walked away, her heart heavy. She hadn't expected to see him, hadn't expected to feel this way. But as she made her way to the bookstore, she realized that maybe coming back to Shimla wasn't just about her father's legacy. Maybe it was about facing the past she had been running from for so long.

And maybe, just maybe, it was about finding a way to move forward.

Unfinished Business

The bells above the door jingled as Meera pushed open the heavy wooden door of the bookstore. She stepped inside, her senses immediately overwhelmed by the familiar scent of old books and wood polish. The store was dark, the blinds drawn, and the dust particles danced lazily in the slivers of sunlight that peeked through the cracks. It was as if time had stood still inside these walls, preserving everything just the way her father had left it.

Meera's eyes wandered around the room, taking in the shelves filled with books of all kinds—some new, some old, some with faded covers and yellowing pages. She had practically grown up in this bookstore, spending countless afternoons curled up in the reading nook, losing herself in stories from faraway lands. It was a place that had always made her feel safe, like she belonged. And now, standing here after all these years, she felt a strange mix of comfort and sorrow.

She slowly made her way to the counter, running her fingers over the familiar grooves in the wood. Her father had stood here every day, greeting customers with a warm smile, recommending books with a passion that was infectious. It was his dream, his pride, and she had always admired him for it. But now that he was gone, the store felt emptier, lonelier, as if it was waiting for her to bring it back to life.

Meera took a deep breath and reminded herself why she was here. She had promised herself she would try to revive the bookstore, keep her father's dream alive. But standing here, surrounded by memories, she wasn't sure if she was strong enough to do it alone.

As she began to clean up, rearranging books and dusting the shelves, her mind drifted back to her unexpected encounter with Raj. She hadn't seen him in almost a decade, and yet there he was, standing in the middle of Mall Road, looking at her with those same warm, brown eyes. It had been so surreal, like stepping into a dream she hadn't quite woken up from. She had thought she was prepared to face him, but the moment she saw him, all her carefully constructed defenses crumbled.

She remembered the way he had looked at her—surprised, but not angry. Kind, but with a hint of sadness. She had so many questions, so many things she wanted to say, but she hadn't been able to find the words. How do you have a conversation with someone who had once been your everything but was now practically a stranger?

Meera was so lost in thought that she didn't hear the door open behind her. It wasn't until she heard a familiar voice that she snapped back to reality.

"Looks like someone's already hard at work."

She turned around to find Raj standing in the doorway, his hands tucked into the pockets of his jacket. He was smiling, but there was a cautiousness in his eyes, as if he wasn't sure how she would react to seeing him again.

"Raj," she said, surprised. "I didn't expect to see you again so soon."

He shrugged, taking a step inside. "I was just passing by and thought I'd check in. I hope you don't mind."

"Of course not," Meera said, quickly gathering her composure. "I'm just trying to clean up a bit. The place needs a lot of work."

Raj looked around the store, his expression thoughtful. "Your dad would be proud. He loved this place more than anything."

"I know," she said quietly. "I just hope I can do it justice."

There was a pause, and for a moment, the only sound was the faint creaking of the floorboards beneath their feet. Raj walked over to one of the shelves, picking up an old, leather-bound book and flipping through its pages. "I used to come here all the time after school, remember? Your dad would always let me borrow books even when I didn't have the money to buy them."

Meera smiled, a wave of nostalgia washing over her. "Yeah, he used to say that books should be read, not just sold. He didn't care about making money, as long as people were reading."

Raj nodded, placing the book back on the shelf. "He had a big heart. It's a rare thing, you know, finding someone who loves what they do as much as he did."

Meera watched him carefully, trying to read his expression. She wondered if he felt the same way she did—like they were standing on the edge of a conversation that needed to happen, but neither of them was brave enough to take the first step.

"How have you been, Raj?" she asked, finally breaking the silence. "It's been a long time."

"It has," he said, his tone soft. "I've been... okay, I guess. Life's been different, that's for sure."

She wanted to ask him so many things. Where had he been? What had he been doing all these years? Why did he never reach out? But she knew that those questions could open up old wounds, and she wasn't sure if she was ready for that.

"Someone told me you're a father now," she said instead, her voice light, even though her heart was heavy.

Raj's face softened, and he smiled. "Yeah. My daughter, Aanya. She's eight now. She's everything to me."

Meera felt a pang in her chest. She hadn't expected to hear that. It was strange, thinking of Raj as a father, imagining him with a little girl who looked up to him. "That's... great. She must be adorable."

"She is," Raj said, his eyes lighting up. "She loves books, too. She's always asking me to bring her new ones. I think she'd love this place."

"You should bring her by sometime," Meera said, surprising herself with how natural it sounded. "I'd like to meet her."

Raj looked at her, his smile fading slightly. "I will. I think she'd like that."

There was another pause, and this time, it felt heavier, as if they were both struggling to find the right words. Meera wanted to ask him about Aanya's mother, about his life now, but she didn't want to overstep. It was strange, having to tiptoe around someone who had once been so close.

"It's good to see you, Meera," Raj said finally, his voice sincere. "I'm glad you're back."

"Thanks," she replied, her throat tightening. "It's good to see you too, Raj."

As he turned to leave, Meera felt a sudden urge to stop him, to ask him to stay a little longer. But she held herself back, letting him walk out the door. She watched as he disappeared down the street, feeling a mix of relief and regret.

She had come back to Shimla to take care of the bookstore, to rebuild her life. But now, she realized that there was something else she needed to confront—something she had been avoiding for too long. Her unfinished business with Raj was still there, lingering between them, waiting to be resolved.

And she wasn't sure if she was ready for that.

CHAPTER THREE

Settling In

The following days were a whirlwind of activity for Meera. She threw herself into cleaning up the bookstore, determined to bring it back to its former glory. Every morning, she'd unlock the door, roll up the shutters, and get to work—dusting shelves, rearranging books, and scrubbing the floors until they gleamed. It was hard work, but it felt good. It gave her a sense of purpose, something she hadn't felt in a long time.

The more time she spent in the store, the more memories resurfaced. She found herself recalling moments from her childhood—her father reading to her in the back room, the two of them sharing a quiet laugh over a cup of tea. Those memories warmed her heart, but they also reminded her of how much she had lost. Still, she pushed through, determined to honor her father's legacy.

One afternoon, as she was stacking a new display of classic novels near the entrance, she heard the door creak open. Meera looked up, expecting to see a customer, but instead, a young girl with curly hair and bright eyes stood in the doorway, clutching a book to her chest. She looked to be around eight years old, with a curious expression on her face.

"Hello," Meera said, smiling. "Can I help you?"

The girl hesitated for a moment, then stepped inside, glancing around the store with wide eyes. "Hi," she said softly. "I was just looking. I love books."

Meera's smile widened. "Well, you've come to the right place. What's your name?"

"Aanya," the girl replied, her voice a little more confident. "My dad said I could come here."

Meera's heart skipped a beat. She hadn't expected this. "Aanya?" she repeated. "Your dad... Raj?"

The girl nodded, a smile spreading across her face. "Do you know him?"

"Yes," Meera said, her voice gentle. "I do."

Aanya looked relieved, as if that piece of information had reassured her. "He said this was the best bookstore in town and that I should come and see it."

"Well, your dad is very smart," Meera said, trying to hide the emotion in her voice. "This was my dad's bookstore. I'm just trying to make it special again."

Aanya beamed, her eyes lighting up. "I like it. It's so... cozy. Like a book from a fairy tale."

Meera felt a warmth spread through her chest. "Thank you, Aanya. That means a lot."

For the next hour, Meera showed Aanya around the store, pointing out different sections, from children's books to fantasy novels. Aanya was enchanted, picking up books at random and asking about them, her enthusiasm infectious. Meera found herself enjoying the girl's company, feeling a sense of ease she hadn't felt in a while.

As they made their way to the children's section, Aanya pulled out a brightly illustrated book. "Can I read this one?" she asked, looking up at Meera with hopeful eyes.

"Of course," Meera said, leading her to a cushioned corner of the store that she was planning to turn into a reading nook. "You can read as many books as you like. This is your space now, too."

Aanya settled down with the book, and for a moment, the store was filled with the sound of her quiet giggles as she turned the pages. Meera watched her, feeling a pang of nostalgia. It was strange how quickly Aanya had made herself at home here, as if she belonged.

Just as she was about to return to her work, the doorbell rang again, and Meera looked up to see Raj standing in the doorway, his hands tucked into his jacket pockets. He seemed surprised to see her, and then his eyes fell on Aanya, who was engrossed in her book.

"There you are," he said, smiling as he walked over to her. "I was wondering where you'd disappeared to."

Aanya looked up, her face lighting up. "Daddy! Look, I found the best book! It has talking animals!"

Raj chuckled, ruffling her hair. "That sounds amazing, sweetheart." Then, he glanced at Meera, his expression softening. "I hope she wasn't bothering you."

"Not at all," Meera said quickly. "She's been a delight. It's nice to have some company."

There was a brief pause as Raj looked around the store, taking in the changes Meera had made. "You've done a great job with the place. It's starting to look like how I remember it."

"I'm trying," Meera said, her voice more vulnerable than she intended. "There's still a lot to do, but... I think it's getting there."

Raj nodded, and for a moment, it felt like they were back in the past, standing in the same spot they had once shared so many conversations. "My dad used to bring me here when I was a kid," he said, his tone nostalgic. "He'd buy me a book every time I got good grades. It's one of my favorite memories."

"Mine too," Meera said softly. "This place was everything to my dad. I just hope I can make it feel like that again."

"I'm sure you will," Raj said, his voice sincere. "If anyone can do it, it's you."

Their eyes met, and Meera felt a strange mix of emotions—comfort, sadness, and a hint of something she couldn't quite name. It was as if they were reconnecting, but there was still a distance between them, a wall built by years of silence and unresolved feelings.

"I'm planning to start some new events," she said, trying to steer the conversation to safer ground. "Book readings, maybe a kids' book club. I think it could bring more people in."

"That sounds like a great idea," Raj said, nodding. "Aanya would love that, wouldn't you, sweetheart?"

Aanya looked up from her book, her eyes shining. "A book club? Really? Can I join?"

Meera laughed. "Of course. You can be our very first member."

Aanya grinned, and for a moment, it was as if the three of them were a little family, sharing a moment of warmth in the cozy bookstore. Meera felt her heart swell, but she quickly pushed the feeling away, reminding herself that this wasn't real. Raj had his own life now, and she was just trying to find her place again.

"Well," Raj said, breaking the silence, "we should get going. But I'll bring her by again if that's okay. She's already in love with this place."

"I'd like that," Meera said, her voice sincere. "It was nice meeting her. And... it was nice seeing you, Raj."

"You too," Raj replied, his gaze lingering on her for a moment before he turned to Aanya. "Come on, kiddo. Let's get home."

Aanya reluctantly closed her book and stood up, waving at Meera. "Bye! I'll come back soon, okay?"

"Okay," Meera said, waving back. "I'll be waiting."

As they left, Meera felt a strange emptiness in the store, as if something precious had been taken away. She hadn't realized how much she missed the feeling of connection, of belonging, until she saw it reflected in Aanya's bright eyes and Raj's gentle smile.

She knew she was opening a door she had kept closed for a long time, but maybe that was okay. Maybe it was time to let the past back in, to see if there was still a place for it in her life. And maybe, just maybe, this bookstore could be the start of something new—for her, for Aanya, and for Raj.

CHAPTER FOUR

Memories and Surprises

The following week was a blur of activity for Meera. She spent her days sorting through old records, cataloging books, and planning events to breathe new life into the bookstore. Despite the hard work, she felt a sense of satisfaction she hadn't felt in years. Every corner she cleaned, every shelf she organized, brought back memories of her father—his patient smile, his deep love for books, and the way he would read aloud to her as a child. It was bittersweet, but it made her feel closer to him, as if he was still there, guiding her.

One morning, as she was unpacking a box of old paperbacks, she found a small, dusty journal wedged between two larger volumes. It was bound in worn brown leather, with yellowed pages and a delicate ribbon marker. Meera's breath hitched as she recognized it—her father's journal. She remembered seeing him jotting down notes in it, but she had never thought much of it at the time.

Curious, she opened the journal and began to flip through the pages. It was filled with her father's neat, cursive handwriting—thoughts, poems, quotes, and little sketches. But as she skimmed through the entries, something caught her eye. There, on one of the pages, was a list of ideas for the bookstore. Her father had written them down like a set of dreams he had hoped to turn into reality—reading events, book swaps, poetry nights. Meera felt a lump form in her throat. These were ideas he had never gotten the chance to implement.

As she continued reading, she found a note scribbled at the bottom of one of the pages, dated a few months before he passed away: *"Meera's Book Club—she doesn't know it yet, but this place will always be hers. Maybe someday she'll see it too."*

Tears pricked at her eyes. She hadn't known how much he had thought about her future, how much he had hoped she would come back. She realized, with a pang of guilt, how she had spent years avoiding Shimla, convincing herself she was too busy, too caught up in her own life. But her father had always believed that this place would be a part of her, no matter where she went.

Wiping her eyes, she closed the journal and placed it carefully on the counter. She took a deep breath and made a decision. She would bring his dreams to life, starting with the book club. It wasn't just about reviving the bookstore anymore—it was about fulfilling her father's wishes, about making him proud.

Later that day, Meera was setting up a new display of children's books when the doorbell jingled, signaling a customer. She glanced up, expecting to see a familiar face, but instead, she was greeted by the sight of an elderly woman with kind, twinkling eyes and a bright pink scarf draped around her shoulders. She was carrying a large basket filled with freshly baked goods.

"Hello there," the woman said, her voice warm. "You must be Meera. I've been hearing all about you."

Meera blinked, momentarily caught off guard. "Yes, that's me. And you are...?"

"I'm Mrs. Sharma," she said with a grin, setting the basket on the counter. "But everyone around here calls me Aunty. I run the little bakery down the street. I used to bake for your father all the time."

Meera's eyes lit up. "Oh! I remember. He would bring home those delicious almond cookies. He was always saying how much he loved them."

Mrs. Sharma's smile softened. "He was a sweet man, your father. I miss him dearly. I've been meaning to come by and see how you were doing. I heard you've been working hard to get this place up and running again."

"I'm trying," Meera said, her voice sincere. "It's been a lot of work, but I want to do it right. For him."

Mrs. Sharma nodded, her eyes full of understanding. "He would be so proud of you, dear. And if there's anything I can do to help, just let me know. In the meantime, I brought you some treats. Consider it a welcome-back gift."

Meera's heart warmed at the gesture. "Thank you, Aunty. That's very kind of you."

As Mrs. Sharma began to unpack the treats—cookies, muffins, and a loaf of freshly baked bread—they chatted about the bookstore and the town. Meera found herself laughing more than she had in days. Mrs. Sharma had a way of making her feel at ease, like she had known her forever. It was a comforting feeling, especially in a place that still felt both familiar and foreign to her.

"So," Mrs. Sharma said, her eyes twinkling mischievously as she arranged the cookies on a small plate, "I heard you had a little run-in with Raj the other day."

Meera felt her cheeks flush. "Word travels fast around here, doesn't it?"

"You bet it does," Mrs. Sharma said with a chuckle. "This is Shimla, after all. But don't worry, everyone's just curious. It's been a while since anyone's seen you two in the same place."

Meera bit her lip, unsure how to respond. She didn't want to get into the details of her past with Raj, especially not with someone she had just met. But Mrs. Sharma seemed to sense her hesitation and quickly changed the subject.

"You know, I'm planning a small event at the bakery this weekend," she said. "A sort of community gathering. I thought it might be a nice way for you to reconnect with some old friends. You should come."

Meera hesitated. The idea of socializing with people she hadn't seen in years made her a little nervous, but at the same time, she knew it could be a good opportunity to spread the word about the bookstore. "That sounds nice. I'll try to make it."

"Good," Mrs. Sharma said, her smile brightening. "And bring some of those flyers you've been putting up. We'll get people talking about the book club."

"Thank you, Aunty," Meera said, genuinely grateful. "I really appreciate it."

As Mrs. Sharma gathered her things and headed out, she paused at the door, turning back to Meera. "And don't be a stranger, okay? Your father was a big part of this community, and so are you. We're all here to support you."

After she left, Meera stood there for a moment, feeling a sense of warmth and gratitude. It was strange how things were slowly falling into place, as if the town was welcoming her back, bit by bit. She felt a little less alone, a little more hopeful.

The weekend arrived faster than Meera expected. She spent the morning at the bookstore, setting up a small display of books to take to Mrs. Sharma's event. As she packed the flyers, she couldn't help but feel a twinge of anxiety. It had been so long since she had been a part of this community. Would people still remember her? Would they welcome her, or would they see her as an outsider?

As she made her way to the bakery, she noticed that the town had come alive with activity. Children ran down the streets, couples strolled hand in hand, and the scent of freshly baked bread filled the air. It was a sight she had missed, even if she hadn't realized it at the time.

When she arrived at the bakery, she was greeted by the sight of a small crowd gathered outside, chatting and laughing. Mrs. Sharma waved her over, her face lighting up when she saw the stack of books in Meera's arms.

"You made it!" she said, giving Meera a warm hug. "And you brought books! That's wonderful. I've already been telling everyone about your new book club."

"Thank you," Meera said, feeling a little less nervous. "I wasn't sure if anyone would be interested, but I'm glad to hear people are talking about it."

"Oh, they're more than interested," Mrs. Sharma said with a wink. "Just wait and see."

As the event got underway, Meera found herself mingling with the crowd, chatting with old acquaintances and making new ones. People were curious about her plans for the bookstore, and to her surprise, many of them seemed genuinely excited about the idea of the book club. It was a small but promising start, and it gave her hope.

Then, as she was handing out flyers, she saw him. Raj was standing near the entrance, talking to a few people, but his eyes were on her. For a moment, their gazes locked, and Meera felt her heart skip a beat. She hadn't expected to see him here, but maybe she shouldn't have been surprised. After all, this was his town too.

He walked over, a smile playing on his lips. "Hey. I see you're making yourself at home."

"I'm trying," Meera said, returning his smile. "Mrs. Sharma has been a big help."

"She tends to do that," Raj said, glancing over at the elderly woman, who was busy serving tea to a group of guests. "I'm glad you came. It's nice to see you out and about."

Meera felt a warmth spread through her chest, and for a moment, she allowed herself to enjoy the feeling. "It's nice to be out," she said softly. "It's starting to feel like home again."

As they stood there, surrounded by the laughter and chatter of the community, Meera realized that maybe this was what she had been missing all along.

CHAPTER FIVE

An Unexpected Offer

The next few days passed quickly for Meera, and the bookstore was beginning to take on a new life. She had set up cozy reading nooks, arranged books by genre, and even hung up a few fairy lights to give the place a warm, welcoming glow. The flyers she had handed out at Mrs. Sharma's event had brought in a few curious visitors, and it felt like things were finally moving in the right direction.

One afternoon, as she was working behind the counter, she heard the familiar jingle of the doorbell. Meera looked up to see a group of women entering the store, chatting animatedly. She recognized a few of them as neighbors she'd seen when she was younger, but she hadn't had a chance to reconnect with them yet.

"Hello, ladies," Meera said, putting on her warmest smile. "Can I help you find anything?"

One of the women, a tall, elegant lady with silver-streaked hair, stepped forward. "Meera, right? We've been hearing all about your plans for the bookstore. We thought we'd come by and see what you've done with the place."

Meera felt a flutter of nerves but kept her smile steady. "I'm glad you did. Feel free to look around."

The women began to explore, murmuring appreciatively as they browsed the shelves. Meera watched them from behind the counter, feeling a mix of excitement and anxiety. These were people who had known her family, who had seen her grow up. She wondered what they thought of her coming back, of her trying to revive something that had been dormant for so long.

After a few minutes, the women gathered near the counter, and the elegant lady, who introduced herself as Mrs. Kapoor, spoke up. "We were talking about your book club idea," she said. "It's wonderful. We've been saying for ages that Shimla needs more places like this—a place where people can come together and share ideas, especially for children. It's good for the community."

Meera's heart swelled with gratitude. "Thank you. I'm hoping to start the book club next month. I want it to be a place where everyone feels welcome."

Mrs. Kapoor nodded approvingly. "I think it's exactly what this town needs. In fact, we were hoping to make a suggestion."

Meera's curiosity was piqued. "Oh? What kind of suggestion?"

"Well," Mrs. Kapoor began, glancing at the other women, who nodded encouragingly, "we were thinking it might be nice to have a small café corner in the bookstore. Just a few tables where people can sit, have a cup of tea or coffee, and maybe a pastry while they read or chat. It would make the place even more inviting."

Meera considered the idea. She had thought about adding a small café area at some point, but it hadn't been a priority. Now, hearing it suggested by someone from the community, it seemed like a logical step. "That's a great idea," she said. "I hadn't planned on doing it right away, but I can definitely look into it."

Mrs. Kapoor smiled, clearly pleased. "I know it's a lot to take on, but I think it could make a real difference. And if you need any help, let us know. My niece runs a small café in town; I'm sure she'd be happy to give you some tips."

Meera's mind was already racing with possibilities. "Thank you so much. I'll definitely keep that in mind."

As the women left, promising to spread the word about the book club, Meera felt a renewed sense of determination. The café idea was ambitious, but it could be exactly what the bookstore needed to draw people in. She made a mental note to reach out to Mrs. Kapoor's niece later in the week.

The next morning, Meera arrived at the bookstore early, eager to start planning. She made a list of potential suppliers for coffee and snacks and began sketching out where she could set up a small café area. She was so engrossed in her work that she didn't hear the door open until a familiar voice interrupted her thoughts.

"You look like you're plotting something serious," Raj said, leaning against the counter with a playful grin.

Meera jumped, startled, and then laughed when she saw who it was. "Raj! You scared me."

"Sorry," he said, though he didn't look particularly sorry. "I just wanted to see how things were going. I hear the whole town is talking about your book club."

"Word travels fast around here," Meera said, shaking her head. "But yes, it's going well. I'm thinking of adding a small café area too. What do you think?"

Raj's eyes lit up. "I think that's a fantastic idea. It's something your dad always wanted to do but never got around to. He used to say that a bookstore should feel like a second home—comfortable, warm, and inviting. Adding a café would be perfect."

Meera felt a pang of emotion at Raj's words. It was still strange to hear him talk about her father, as if no time had passed. "I wish I had known that," she said softly. "I found his journal the other day, and it made me realize how much he had planned for this place. It feels like I'm just catching up now."

Raj's expression softened. "You're doing more than catching up, Meera. You're making it your own. And that's what he would have wanted."

Meera didn't know how to respond to that. She was grateful for Raj's support, but it was also a reminder of how much things had changed between them. Before she could dwell on it, Raj pulled a small envelope out of his jacket pocket and handed it to her.

"What's this?" she asked, taking it.

"Open it," he said, his eyes twinkling.

Meera carefully opened the envelope and found a handwritten invitation inside. It was for a small charity event, a fundraiser for a local children's home. The event was being hosted at the town hall, and there was a note at the bottom that read: *Special reading session by Meera Singh.*

Meera looked up at Raj, confused. "Did you...?"

"I thought it might be a good way to promote the bookstore," he said quickly. "You'd be reading a children's story to the kids, and afterwards, we could hand out flyers for the book club. Plus, it's for a good cause."

"I don't know, Raj," Meera said hesitantly. "I'm not really good at public speaking."

"You don't have to be," he said, his tone gentle. "Just be yourself. The kids will love you. And I'll be there to support you."

Meera bit her lip, considering it. The idea of reading to a group of children, especially in public, made her a little nervous. But she also knew it was a great opportunity to introduce the bookstore to more people. And if Raj thought she could do it, maybe she could.

"Okay," she said finally. "I'll do it."

Raj's smile widened, and for a moment, Meera felt like they were back in college, planning events and working together. "Great. I'll make sure everything is set up. It'll be fun, I promise."

As Raj left, Meera felt a mix of excitement and anxiety. She hadn't done anything like this in a long time, and the thought of standing in front of a crowd made her stomach twist. But she also felt a spark of determination. This was her chance to show the town what the bookstore could be—a place of warmth, community, and connection.

The day of the charity event arrived faster than Meera expected. She spent the morning practicing her reading, trying to memorize the story she had chosen—a charming tale about a brave little squirrel who finds her way back home after getting lost in the woods. The story felt personal, like a metaphor for her own journey, and she hoped the kids would enjoy it.

When she arrived at the town hall, she was greeted by the sight of colorful decorations, balloons, and a stage set up for the reading. There was already a small crowd gathering, and Meera felt her nerves spike. She spotted Raj near the entrance, talking to some of the organizers, and he waved her over.

"You made it," he said, his smile reassuring. "Are you ready?"

"As ready as I'll ever be," she said, trying to sound more confident than she felt.

"Don't worry," he said, giving her a gentle nudge. "You're going to be great. Just imagine you're reading to Aanya. She's been talking about it all week."

Meera's heart softened at the mention of Aanya. She hadn't seen the little girl since their last encounter at the bookstore, but knowing she was excited to hear her read made Meera feel a bit more confident.

The event began with a few speeches, and then it was time for Meera's reading. She took a deep breath as she stepped onto the stage, feeling the weight of dozens of eyes on her. But as she looked out at the crowd, she saw Aanya sitting in the front row, beaming up at her. Next to her was Raj, his expression calm and encouraging.

Meera began to read, her voice a little shaky at first, but as she got into the story, she found herself relaxing. The children were captivated, their eyes wide with wonder as they listened to the tale of the brave little squirrel. By the time she finished, the room was filled with applause, and Meera felt a wave of relief and joy.

CHAPTER SIX

A Taste of the Past

The warmth of Aanya's hug lingered long after the charity event ended. For Meera, it was more than just a successful reading; it was a step closer to reestablishing her roots in Shimla. She had spent years trying to build a life elsewhere, but now, surrounded by the community, she felt something she hadn't felt in a long time—a sense of belonging.

The rest of the event was a blur of friendly conversations and smiles. Many parents came up to her, thanking her for the reading and expressing interest in the book club. It seemed Raj's idea had worked; she now had a growing list of names to contact once she officially launched the club. The organizers even offered her a chance to set up a small stall at future events, where she could showcase books from the store.

As Meera packed up her things, she noticed Raj talking with a group of volunteers. He looked relaxed, chatting and laughing as he helped clear up the decorations. Watching him from a distance, she was reminded of the easy, effortless way they used to be around each other. Things were different now—there was a gap between them that hadn't been there before—but for a moment, she allowed herself to remember what it had been like.

Just as she was about to leave, Raj walked over, his eyes bright with excitement. "You did it," he said, sounding genuinely impressed. "I knew you would, but that was even better than I expected."

"Thanks," Meera said, feeling a little shy under his praise. "I was so nervous at first, but then I saw Aanya and... I don't know, it just got easier."

Raj's smile softened. "She's a good kid. And she adores you, by the way. She hasn't stopped talking about you since you met."

Meera blushed. "She's adorable. I'm glad she liked the story."

There was a pause, a moment of silence that felt heavy with unspoken words. Meera hesitated, then decided to take a chance. "Raj... I was thinking, maybe we could catch up sometime. You know, outside of bookstore stuff."

Raj's eyes flickered with surprise, but he quickly recovered, nodding. "I'd like that. How about tonight? There's a place I know that has the best chai and pakoras. We could go there, just like old times."

"Tonight?" Meera echoed, slightly taken aback. "That's... yeah, okay. That sounds nice."

A few hours later, Meera found herself standing outside a small, cozy café nestled in one of Shimla's quieter lanes. It was a place she hadn't been to in years, and stepping inside felt like stepping back in time. The café hadn't changed much—dim lights, the scent of spices and tea leaves, and the same wooden tables she remembered from her college days.

Raj was already there, sitting at a corner table with two cups of steaming chai in front of him. When he saw her, he stood up and waved, grinning like a teenager. "I took the liberty of ordering for us. Hope you don't mind."

"Not at all," Meera said as she sat down. She picked up the cup, letting the warmth seep into her hands, and took a sip. The taste was perfect, just as she remembered. "I can't believe this place is still here. It feels like nothing's changed."

Raj leaned back, his eyes reflecting the dim light. "Some things don't. This café, for one. And some things do," he added, his gaze lingering on her.

Meera felt a flutter in her chest. "Yeah, I guess so."

For a while, they sipped their tea in comfortable silence, the hum of quiet conversations around them creating a soothing backdrop. Then Raj spoke up, his tone more serious. "I've been thinking about what you said, about catching up. I know it's been a long time, and there's a lot we haven't talked about... but I'm glad you're back, Meera. I didn't realize how much I missed having you around until I saw you again."

Meera's heart tightened. There it was, the gap between them, laid bare. She had been avoiding this conversation, afraid of what it might bring up, but she knew they couldn't keep dancing around it forever. "I missed you too, Raj," she said quietly. "But a lot has changed. We're not the same people we were back then."

"I know," he said, leaning forward, his eyes searching hers. "But maybe that's okay. Maybe we can get to know each other again."

Meera didn't know what to say. Part of her wanted to leap at the chance, to let herself believe that they could pick up where they left off. But another part of her was cautious, afraid of getting hurt again. "It's not that simple, Raj."

"Maybe not," he agreed, his tone gentle. "But I'm willing to try if you are."

She looked down at her cup, tracing the rim with her finger. She thought about the bookstore, her father's journal, and the way Raj had been there, quietly supporting her every step of the way. Maybe he was right. Maybe they could try again, one step at a time. "Okay," she said finally, looking up at him with a small smile. "Let's try."

Raj's face lit up, and for the first time in a long while, Meera felt a sense of hope, like a small, flickering light in the dark.

The next day, as Meera unlocked the bookstore and stepped inside, she was greeted by the familiar scent of old books and polished wood. She had a long list of things to do—inventory, arranging the new books she'd ordered, and finalizing the plans for the book club—but she felt lighter than she had in days. Last night with Raj had been... nice. Easier than she'd expected. Maybe they really could find a way to rebuild their friendship, one conversation at a time.

She had just started arranging a new display of children's books when the doorbell jingled. Meera glanced up, expecting to see a customer, but instead, she found herself face to face with Mrs. Kapoor, who was carrying a large, colorful basket.

"Good morning, Meera!" Mrs. Kapoor said cheerfully, setting the basket down on the counter. "I brought you something."

"Oh, wow, thank you," Meera said, peering into the basket. It was filled with jars of homemade pickles, chutneys, and a few small, beautifully wrapped packages. "What's all this?"

"Just a little something from the ladies' group," Mrs. Kapoor said with a wink. "We've been talking, and we wanted to help with your café idea. Consider this a small contribution to get you started. The chutneys are my specialty, and I think they'd go perfectly with a nice cup of tea."

Meera was touched by the gesture. "This is so kind of you. I wasn't expecting anything like this."

"Well, we believe in what you're doing," Mrs. Kapoor said, her expression softening. "Your father did so much for this town, and we're glad to see you bringing the bookstore back to life. Besides, who doesn't love a good cup of chai and a snack to go with it?"

Meera laughed, feeling a warmth spread through her chest. "Thank you. Really, this means a lot."

As Mrs. Kapoor left, Meera placed the basket on the counter and looked around the store. She could almost imagine her father standing there, smiling, his eyes twinkling with pride. For the first time since she had returned, she felt like she was exactly where she was meant to be.

Later that afternoon, as she was updating the store's social media page, she received a message from Raj. It was a simple text: *Free this evening? Thought we could brainstorm more café ideas.*

Meera hesitated, her fingers hovering over the keyboard. They had agreed to try, but she still felt that familiar mix of excitement and caution. Finally, she typed back: *Sure. Meet at the bookstore?*

Raj's reply came almost immediately: *Sounds good. I'll bring the chai.*

Meera smiled, shaking her head. She could already imagine him walking in with a thermos, ready to chat about everything from café menus to book club themes. As she set her phone down, she thought about how strange it was that, despite everything, Raj still had the power to make her feel like a teenager—nervous, hopeful, and just a little bit thrilled.

As the sun began to set, casting a warm, golden light across the bookstore, Meera took a moment to savor the peace of the moment. She didn't know what the future held for her or for the bookstore, but for the first time in a long time, she was ready to find out.

CHAPTER SEVEN

A Spark Ignited

Meera watched as the last traces of daylight melted into dusk, filling the bookstore with a warm, cozy glow. It was past closing time, but she didn't mind waiting a little longer. Raj would be there soon, and the thought of spending the evening with him brought a quiet thrill that she hadn't felt in years.

True to his word, Raj arrived with a thermos of chai and a bag of samosas from the café where they'd shared chai the night before. He greeted her with his usual easy grin, and Meera felt a flutter of excitement as he entered the store.

"Thought I'd bring something to go with the chai," he said, holding up the bag. "I remember you used to love these."

Meera smiled, taking the bag and inhaling the familiar, spicy aroma. "You remembered," she said softly, glancing up at him. It was a small thing, but it meant something to her that he remembered her favorites.

"Of course I remember," he said, his voice dropping to a gentle tone. "Some things don't change, right?"

They moved to the back of the store, where Meera had set up a few comfortable chairs near a shelf filled with classics. The warmth from the dim lights above created a cozy nook, the perfect spot to unwind and brainstorm.

"So," Raj began as they settled in, pouring chai into two cups. "Mrs. Kapoor told me she came by earlier. Seems like the whole town is rooting for this café idea of yours."

Meera took a sip of her chai, feeling the warmth spread through her. "It was so kind of her. She even brought pickles and chutneys for me to use. I hadn't thought about the café seriously before, but now... now it feels like the right thing to do."

Raj nodded, taking a bite of his samosa. "I think it's perfect. Shimla's needed a place like this for a long time. Plus, it'll set your bookstore apart. People will come here not just for books but for the atmosphere, the experience."

Meera's gaze drifted around the store, imagining what it would look like with a few small tables, maybe a counter with pastries and tea. She could almost picture people sitting here, lost in books or in quiet conversation. "I just want this place to feel like a second home for people," she said softly. "A place where they can come to relax, to be themselves."

Raj looked at her, a hint of admiration in his eyes. "I think you're already making that happen. I mean, look at this place. It's coming alive, Meera. You're bringing a piece of yourself into it, and people feel that."

Meera's heart swelled at his words. She hadn't thought about it that way before, but he was right. The bookstore was more than just a project; it was a reflection of her dreams, her memories, her father's legacy. It was her own way of creating something meaningful.

They spent the next hour brainstorming ideas, laughing as they threw out suggestions for café names and menu items. Raj had an almost childlike enthusiasm, suggesting everything from "Novel Brews" to "Chapter & Chai." Meera found herself laughing, genuinely laughing, in a way she hadn't in ages. It felt easy, natural, as if no time had passed between them.

As their laughter faded, a comfortable silence settled over them. Raj leaned back, gazing at her thoughtfully. "You know," he began, his voice softer, "I've missed this. Just... sitting with you, talking about ideas. It feels like old times."

Meera looked down, her cheeks warming under his gaze. She knew what he meant. There was a familiarity between them, a bond that felt stronger than the years they had spent apart. "I missed it too," she admitted. "Sometimes I think about those days in college... how simple everything felt."

Raj sighed, a faraway look in his eyes. "Those were good days. But, you know, it's not so bad now either."

She looked up, meeting his gaze, and for a moment, the space between them felt electric. There was something in his eyes, something she had seen only a handful of times—a vulnerability, a hint of longing. Meera's heart quickened, but before she could dwell on it, he looked away, breaking the moment.

Raj cleared his throat, shifting back to their conversation. "Anyway, I think we have a solid plan here. Once you start the café, this place is going to take off. You'll have book readings, community events... it'll be like a little cultural hub for Shimla."

Meera nodded, grateful for the change in subject but still feeling the remnants of that fleeting moment. "Thank you, Raj. For everything. I don't think I could have done this without you."

"You don't have to thank me," he said, giving her a reassuring smile. "I want to help. This place, it's important to you, and that makes it important to me too."

They spent a few more minutes discussing practicalities—suppliers, pricing, logistics—before the conversation wound down. The store was quiet now, the evening's chill seeping in through the windows. Meera looked at her watch, surprised at how quickly the time had passed.

"Guess we got a bit carried away," she said with a laugh, standing up to gather the cups and napkins.

Raj stood too, reaching for his coat. "Time flies when you're having fun, right?"

As they moved toward the front of the store, Meera felt a sudden pang of reluctance. She didn't want the evening to end. But as Raj turned to face her, something in his expression gave her pause.

"Meera," he began, his voice hesitant. "There's something I've been wanting to say."

Her heart skipped a beat. She wasn't sure what he was going to say, but she could feel the weight of it.

"I know we've both changed," he continued, his gaze steady on hers. "And I know things weren't easy between us. But seeing you here, working on this bookstore, being a part of this community... it's reminded me of why we were close in the first place. You have this way of making people feel at home, of creating a sense of belonging. And that's... that's something I haven't found anywhere else."

Meera felt her throat tighten, her emotions swirling. She had spent so long guarding her heart, telling herself that the past was behind her. But hearing Raj's words, seeing the sincerity in his eyes, stirred something in her that she thought she had buried.

"I feel the same way, Raj," she whispered, barely able to meet his gaze. "Being back here, it's brought up a lot of old memories. But it's also made me realize that... maybe it's okay to open up again, to let people in."

Raj's hand brushed against hers, a simple, fleeting touch that sent a jolt of warmth through her. "I don't want to rush anything," he said gently. "But if there's a chance, even a small one, that we could start over... I'd like to take it."

Meera's heart raced, and for a moment, she allowed herself to imagine it—a future with Raj, a fresh start filled with laughter, warmth, and shared dreams. She didn't know what lay ahead, but in that moment, she felt a spark of hope, like a light piercing through the darkness.

"Let's take it slow," she said, a soft smile playing on her lips. "One step at a time."

Raj smiled back, his eyes shining with a mix of relief and joy. "One step at a time," he agreed, his voice filled with quiet determination.

As he left, Meera stood by the door, watching him disappear into the night. The store felt different now, infused with a newfound sense of possibility. She turned off the lights, locking up and stepping into the crisp Shimla air. She wrapped her scarf around herself, feeling a warmth that had nothing to do with the fabric.

And for the first time in a long while, she allowed herself to believe in second chances.

CHAPTER EIGHT

A Shared Journey

The following morning dawned crisp and clear, sunlight pouring through the bookstore's windows and illuminating the shelves. Meera was already setting up, arranging the new books and preparing the store for the day's customers. But even in the quiet of the early morning, her mind buzzed with thoughts of the previous night.

Raj's words had left her with a strange mix of exhilaration and nervousness. A second chance was something she hadn't allowed herself to imagine. And now, here it was, presenting itself slowly and gently, like the first signs of spring. She found herself smiling as she arranged the books, wondering if it was possible to rebuild what they had once shared.

Lost in her thoughts, she was startled when the doorbell jingled. Looking up, she saw Mrs. Kapoor bustling in, holding a thick binder in her arms and wearing her usual cheerful smile.

"Good morning, Meera!" she greeted, placing the binder on the counter with a flourish. "I've brought you something to help with the café. Consider it a little gift from the ladies' group."

Curious, Meera opened the binder to find it filled with handwritten recipes, each page decorated with little doodles and notes. There were recipes for teas and snacks, chutneys and pickles, even a few dessert ideas. "Mrs. Kapoor, this is amazing!" Meera exclaimed, touched by the effort.

"It's a community project," Mrs. Kapoor said, clearly pleased with Meera's reaction. "Each of us has contributed our own family recipes. We thought it would be nice if the café offered traditional flavors—things we grew up with, things that bring back memories."

Meera felt a surge of gratitude as she flipped through the pages. "Thank you so much. This is exactly what I wanted—a place that feels like home, with food that brings people together."

Mrs. Kapoor winked. "That's the spirit! And of course, we'll all come by to taste-test, so you'll have a loyal crowd from day one!"

They chatted for a while longer, discussing the logistics of the café and the upcoming book club launch. As Mrs. Kapoor left, promising to return soon with more volunteers, Meera felt a renewed sense of purpose. She could feel the community's support wrapping around her, like a warm embrace.

Later that afternoon, Raj dropped by, carrying a large box filled with fresh mugs and teacups. "For the café," he said with a grin as he set the box down. "Picked these up from a local potter. Thought they'd add a nice personal touch."

Meera lifted one of the mugs, admiring the rustic, handcrafted design. "These are beautiful, Raj. Thank you."

Raj shrugged, smiling. "I figured we should support local artists too. Plus, each piece is unique, just like your bookstore."

They spent the rest of the afternoon unpacking and arranging the mugs, discussing possible names for the café and deciding where to set up the tables. With every little decision, Meera felt Raj's support and excitement, and it warmed her heart to see him so involved. They were creating something special together, something that felt both familiar and new.

As they worked, Raj paused, a thoughtful look crossing his face. "Hey, Meera, remember that spot we used to go to just outside of town? By the lake?"

Meera looked up, surprised. Of course she remembered—the hidden lake, nestled between the trees, had been their secret escape during college. It was where they'd shared dreams, plans, and late-night laughter.

"Yes, I remember," she said softly. "I haven't been there in years."

Raj hesitated, then smiled. "Why don't we go? I mean, after we finish up here. It'll be like a little trip down memory lane."

Meera felt a flicker of excitement. The lake had always held a special place in her heart, and the idea of revisiting it with Raj filled her with both nostalgia and anticipation. "Okay," she agreed. "I'd like that."

By late afternoon, they were on the road, winding through the narrow paths and dense forests of Shimla's outskirts. Raj drove with ease, navigating the familiar curves as if no time had passed. The air was crisp and fresh, carrying the scent of pine trees and damp earth.

As they neared the lake, Meera felt a rush of memories. They used to come here often, escaping the pressures of college life to find peace by the water. It was their place, a haven where the world felt distant and unimportant.

When they finally arrived, Meera stepped out of the car and took a deep breath, letting the tranquility wash over her. The lake was just as she remembered—serene and still, reflecting the clear blue sky and the surrounding trees. A few birds chirped nearby, and the gentle rustle of leaves filled the silence.

"It's beautiful," she murmured, turning to Raj, who was watching her with a soft smile.

"It always was," he replied, his voice barely above a whisper. He walked closer to the water, hands in his pockets, as if he, too, was caught up in the memories.

They sat on a rock near the shore, side by side, watching the water ripple in the breeze. For a while, neither of them spoke, each lost in their own thoughts. Finally, Raj broke the silence.

"Coming here with you... it feels like things haven't changed," he said quietly. "But at the same time, everything's different."

Meera nodded, understanding exactly what he meant. "We've both been through a lot," she said. "Life happened, and we drifted apart. But... I'm glad we found our way back here."

Raj looked down, picking up a small pebble and tossing it into the lake. "Do you ever wonder what would have happened if we hadn't gone our separate ways?"

Meera hesitated, feeling a pang of sadness. "Sometimes. But I try not to dwell on it. We both needed time to grow, to figure out who we are."

He nodded, but she could see a flicker of regret in his eyes. "I used to think that way too. But seeing you again, being back in Shimla... it makes me wish things had been different."

A heavy silence settled between them, filled with years of unspoken words and lingering emotions. Meera felt her heart ache, both for the past and the possibility of a future that might never be. But as she looked at Raj, she realized that she didn't want to live with regrets anymore.

"Maybe it's not too late," she said softly, her voice barely audible.

Raj turned to her, his expression hopeful. "Do you mean that?"

She nodded, a small smile tugging at her lips. "I think we have a chance to start over, if we're both willing to try."

A warm smile spread across Raj's face, and he reached for her hand, holding it gently. They sat there, hand in hand, watching the sun dip lower in the sky, casting a golden glow over the lake. It felt like a new beginning, a promise of what could be.

As the sun began to set, Meera felt a sense of peace settle over her. She didn't know what the future held, but for the first time, she was ready to embrace it, to take a leap of faith and let go of the past. Together, they stood, walking back to the car hand in hand, their footsteps light with the weight of burdens finally lifted.

On the drive back, the silence between them was comfortable, filled with a quiet joy. Meera looked out at the familiar landscape, feeling a deep sense of gratitude for the journey that had brought her back here, to this moment.

When they arrived at the bookstore, Raj walked her to the door, lingering for a moment before saying goodnight. As he left, Meera watched him disappear into the night, a soft smile on her lips. She felt a spark of hope, a quiet assurance that maybe, just maybe, they could rewrite their story.

CHAPTER NINE

The Road Less Taken

The following days passed in a delightful haze for Meera. The plans for the café were progressing beautifully, with help from Raj and the occasional cheerful drop-in from Mrs. Kapoor and the other ladies of the town. Meera found herself buzzing with ideas, inspiration, and a growing sense of belonging, not only to the community but also to Raj's world once again.

It was late afternoon when Meera was rearranging a display shelf in the bookstore. The tinkling bell on the door announced Raj's arrival, and she looked up to find him smiling, holding a small bouquet of wildflowers he must have gathered on his way over.

"For you," he said, handing her the flowers.

Meera smiled, taking in the earthy, fresh scent. "These are beautiful, thank you. Where did you find them?"

"Up near the old hiking trail," he replied, leaning casually against a shelf. "I thought they'd add a bit of color to the store."

She placed the flowers in a small glass jar on the counter, feeling her heart lighten with his simple gesture. "They're perfect."

Raj grinned. "Speaking of the old trail, I was thinking... how about a little adventure? Just you and me, like old times."

Meera hesitated, feeling the familiar thrill of their college days—spontaneous hikes, hidden trails, and the thrill of discovering new places together. "A hike? Now?"

"Why not? You need a break. And trust me, the view is worth it. Besides," he added, his voice teasing, "it might give us some ideas for the café. Outdoor seating, maybe?"

She laughed, glancing around the quiet bookstore. She'd been pouring her energy into the café lately, but a change of scenery sounded like exactly what she needed. "Alright, I'll grab my things!"

They drove up the winding road that led to the trailhead, the air growing crisper as they ascended. Raj's car bumped along the path, their laughter filling the spaces between the trees. When they finally arrived, Meera looked out over the dense green forest, the expanse of mountains stretching out against the sky. She'd forgotten how stunning it was up here, the untouched beauty of Shimla's landscape.

"Feels good to be out here," she said, stepping out of the car and breathing in the fresh air.

Raj nodded, slinging a small backpack over his shoulder. "This place has always been special. Ready for a bit of a hike?"

They set off along the narrow trail, the crunch of leaves underfoot and the occasional chirp of birds accompanying them. They walked in companionable silence, sometimes exchanging memories of their past hikes, sometimes simply enjoying the tranquility.

After a while, they reached a viewpoint overlooking a wide valley. The sun was beginning to set, casting a warm, amber glow over the landscape. Raj took a seat on a large rock, gesturing for Meera to join him.

She settled beside him, and they both gazed out at the breathtaking view. Shimla lay below them, the small town nestled in the valley, lights beginning to flicker on as dusk approached.

"I missed this place," Meera murmured, almost to herself. "When I was away, I would think about it sometimes, especially on stressful days. There's a peace here that I could never find anywhere else."

Raj glanced at her, his expression soft. "I used to feel the same way. But I think it was more than just this place that I missed. It was the people, the memories..." He hesitated, then added, "It was you."

The words hung in the air, and Meera felt a warmth spread through her. She'd sensed the change between them, the slow rekindling of something long buried, but hearing him say it so openly made her heart skip.

"I feel like I left a part of myself here," she said softly, looking out at the horizon. "Coming back feels like picking up pieces of who I used to be."

Raj's hand found hers, resting lightly atop it. "You're still the same Meera, though. The one who can't stop rearranging her bookshelf or remember all the little details of everyone's lives."

Meera laughed, the sound a soft echo in the quiet of the forest. "I guess some things never change."

They sat in silence, hand in hand, each lost in their thoughts. Finally, Raj spoke. "Meera, I know we're trying to take things slow. But there's something I want you to know."

She turned to him, her heart pounding softly in her chest. His gaze was steady, his voice quiet but filled with a sincerity that made her breath catch.

"Being here with you, helping with the café, sharing these little moments... it's made me realize how much I've missed you," he said. "And I don't want to pretend that I'm not falling for you all over again."

Meera's cheeks warmed, and she felt an overwhelming mix of emotions—happiness, hope, and a twinge of fear. She had kept her heart guarded for so long, but with Raj, those walls seemed to crumble, little by little.

"I'm scared too, Raj," she admitted, her voice barely a whisper. "But I want to try. I want to see where this goes."

He smiled, relief and joy evident in his expression. "Then let's take that road, together."

They watched the sun sink lower, casting hues of pink and orange across the sky, illuminating the valley in a magical glow. In that moment, with Raj beside her, Meera felt a peace and excitement she hadn't known in years. The future was uncertain, but for once, she was willing to embrace it.

As they walked back down the trail, Raj's hand slipped into hers, and they shared stories and laughter as they retraced their steps. By the time they returned to the car, dusk had fully settled, and a soft, silvery moon hung in the sky.

Back in town, they stopped for chai at a small roadside stall, sipping the warm tea and enjoying the quiet of the night. Meera leaned back in her chair, watching the moonlight dance on the mountains.

Raj glanced at her, a thoughtful look in his eyes. "You know, Meera, this café idea—it feels like something big, something special. I think it's going to be more than just a café."

She nodded, smiling softly. "I hope so. I want it to be a place where people can feel at home, where they can escape their worries and just be. Like the lake, or this trail. A sanctuary."

Raj took her hand, giving it a gentle squeeze. "With you behind it, I have no doubt it'll be all that and more."

They stayed at the stall for a while, talking and sipping their tea, until the night grew late and the town quieted. When Raj finally dropped her off at the bookstore, he walked her to the door, pausing before saying goodbye.

"Today was perfect," he said, his voice soft. "Thank you for sharing it with me."

Meera felt her heart swell as she met his gaze. "It was. Thank you, too."

They stood there, neither wanting to leave, until finally, Raj leaned in and kissed her cheek, his touch warm and gentle. "Goodnight, Meera."

"Goodnight, Raj," she whispered, watching him walk away, his figure disappearing into the night.

As she locked up and headed inside, Meera's thoughts lingered on their day together, on the shared laughter and the warmth of Raj's hand in hers. She felt her heart flutter, a hope blossoming within her. Perhaps, just perhaps, this was the beginning of a new chapter—one where she and Raj could create a story all their own.

CHAPTER TEN

A New Chapter

The grand opening of the café arrived on a chilly autumn morning, with golden sunlight streaming through the trees. Meera arrived early to make the final touches, her heart beating with a mix of excitement and nerves. The café tables were arranged along the bookstore's front and side, each one set with the handmade pottery mugs Raj had found and vases filled with fresh wildflowers. The aroma of chai, brewed with Mrs. Kapoor's special spice blend, wafted through the air, blending with the scent of books and freshly baked samosas.

Raj was already there, hanging the new café sign just above the door. "The Reading Nook & Café," it read in simple, elegant lettering, with smaller words beneath it: "A place to pause, read, and belong."

He turned as Meera approached, a grin spreading across his face. "I think it looks perfect, don't you?"

She smiled, feeling a warmth spread through her at the sight of him. "Better than I imagined. Thank you for all of this, Raj. I couldn't have done it without you."

They shared a long, meaningful look before the noise of guests arriving pulled them back to the present. The town's residents began trickling in, Mrs. Kapoor at the front, her friends trailing behind her, all of them beaming with excitement.

"Oh, it's just lovely!" she exclaimed, clapping her hands in delight. "You've outdone yourself, Meera. And, Raj, we're so proud of you both!"

Raj chuckled, exchanging a quick, happy glance with Meera. "Thank you, Mrs. Kapoor. We're glad you're here to celebrate with us."

The morning rolled on as the guests settled in with mugs of tea and plates of sweets. Meera moved between tables, greeting familiar faces, listening to their stories, and sharing the joy of finally seeing her dream come to life. A quiet happiness filled her as she saw people laughing, swapping books, and chatting with each other. The café felt alive, as though it had always been a part of the bookstore, waiting for this moment.

Raj found her as the crowd began to thin, offering her a cup of tea as they took a seat by the window.

"I've been meaning to tell you," he began, a shy smile on his face. "There's something that's been on my mind."

Meera's heart skipped as she looked at him, curious. "What is it?"

He took a deep breath, his gaze steady. "Being here with you, helping with the café, seeing everything come together—it's made me realize that this is where I belong, Meera. With you, here in Shimla. And I don't want this to end."

The weight of his words settled between them, filling her with a joy that felt both thrilling and peaceful.

"Raj... I feel the same," she whispered, her voice filled with emotion. "I came back to Shimla to find myself again, but being with you has shown me so much more than I could've imagined. I don't want to go back to being apart. Not again."

Raj smiled, his eyes warm and filled with hope. "Then let's make this our beginning. Together."

She reached for his hand, and they sat there in quiet understanding, watching the last of the guests linger over their tea. Mrs. Kapoor waved goodbye as she left, and soon the bookstore fell into a peaceful silence, just the two of them remaining.

After they closed for the day, Meera and Raj walked along the town's narrow streets, their hands entwined. The sky was a deep shade of indigo, stars beginning to blink to life above the mountains. They strolled past familiar landmarks, down the same roads they'd walked as young college students, now sharing dreams that were bigger, wiser, and somehow more vibrant.

When they reached the lake, they paused to watch the moonlight reflecting off the still water. Standing beside him in the silence of the night, Meera felt a deep sense of belonging, not only to Shimla but to Raj and the life they were building together. She leaned her head against his shoulder, and he wrapped his arm around her, holding her close.

"It's funny," she murmured, her voice barely louder than a whisper. "I came back here searching for answers, and instead, I found you."

Raj tilted her face up to meet his gaze, his expression tender. "We found each other," he said softly, brushing a strand of hair from her face. "And that's all that matters."

Under the vast, star-studded sky, they shared a gentle, unhurried kiss, one that spoke of promises and possibilities. It felt like the end of an old story and the beginning of something new—a love that was built on shared memories and future dreams.

As they walked back toward the town, the lights from the café twinkling in the distance, Meera felt her heart overflowing with gratitude. This was her home, her community, her love—and she knew, without a doubt, that her story had come full circle. With Raj by her side, they would fill the coming chapters with joy, laughter, and love, writing a story that was theirs alone.

www.ingramcontent.com/pod-product-compliance
Lightning Source LLC
Chambersburg PA
CBHW031243130726
47988CB00008B/3216